SANITARY SQUAD

PIPES OF WAR

MEET THE SQUAD

Captain Clean
Clifford Cane
(The leader)

HyJean
Jean Wilkes
(The genius)

Faucet
Nelson Spigot
(The superpower)

Flush
Will Armitage
(The part-timer)

Sgt. Suds
Mick Goldman
(The muscle)

Mary
(The administrator)

Filtham. A city just outside London, but far enough that they didn't have to increase the prices of their hot beverages to trick unsuspecting tourists. It was a small city; historically unimportant, but a few famous writers and sports people had been born there – before quickly moving to London when they realised it was much nicer and had better coffee. The city of Filtham seemed to live up to its name, with barely a see-through window in sight along the well-littered streets. No matter how much people cleaned, it always seemed to revert back to a less than welcoming state. But one place that was cleaner than most was the shopping centre. Filtham Shopping Centre was the heart of the city. Partly because it had a wide range of shops and restaurants to offer retail and nourishment, but also because there were plenty of regular beatings going on. This was mainly due to drunken parties who had wandered over from local bars at night when Filtham City Football Club (or "FC squared" as the locals referred to it, which in turn led to rival fans nicknaming it "FC scared") lost a match – which was unfortunately quite a regular occurrence. But aside from the occasional hooliganism, it was a fairly ordinary shopping centre. Trendy clothes shops, expensive electronic shops, too many artisan coffee shops and not enough escalators. Least important were the toilets – unless you were desperate, in which case they suddenly became the most important place in the shopping centre. On the second floor, tucked away next to a women's clothes shop, were the public toilets. Inside, on one particular day, a man called Chad Baker zipped up his flies and did his usual little post-wee whistle. He was a young, handsome guy, dressed in trendy clothes. In years gone by, he would've been described as a yuppie, but these days people had other, less polite names they would use.

'See you out there,' he said to his equally despisable friend, who was still in the middle of relieving himself at the urinal. Chad made his way towards the door, heading back out into the crowded shopping centre to continue buying things he didn't need just because he could afford them. He eyed himself up in the mirror as he passed, admiring his reflection with a self-assured grin. However, as he turned to leave, a hand suddenly reached out and slammed against the door, pushing it shut. Slowly and silently, the hand reached down and turned the lock, trapping the three of them inside.

Chad stumbled back in surprise and watched as the mysterious doorman stepped out of the shadows. He was a tall, well-built man, who was muscular but still had a bit of a 'dad bod', dressed in a blue shirt and jeans, along with a pair of marigold gloves and a matching yellow bed sheet tied around his neck. But most surprising was his face, or rather the lack of one. His head was completely concealed in toilet paper, wrapped around like a modern-day mummy, with only a small gap showing his dark eyes, staring menacingly at Chad.

'Yurph durphum rursh yurh hurph,' mumbled the man.

'Wh-what?' asked Chad, a slight quiver in his voice as he took a step backwards.

'Yuph durph… hurph urmph,' he raised a gloved hand and pulled a bit of the toilet roll away from his face to reveal his mouth. 'You didn't wash your hands,' he said in a deep, gruff voice that sounded like he'd just swallowed a bag of gravel.

Chad stood up a bit straighter, some of his confidence returning after hearing the less than threatening accusation. 'Yeah, so what?' he scoffed.

'Don't you know there's a virus going around,' said the man. 'You're spreading your germs among all those people out there.'

'Who cares? I ain't got no virus,' said Chad, moving forward to try and push past the crazy man.

However, the crazy man stopped him and pushed him back with a surprisingly strong shove.

'You might have it and not know it!' he shouted angrily. 'You could pass it on to anyone! And even if you don't, you'll still be spreading around your germs! Now wash your hands!'

'Hey, leave him alone freak!' came a voice from behind. Chad's friend – who had been struggling to finish at the urinal while all this was going on – ran forward and took a swing at the man. Little did he know, the masked man was actually an expert in several martial arts. He dodged the swinging arm and threw his own punch at the kid's face, knocking him back down onto to the floor.

'Now wash your hands!' he repeated to Chad in his gravelly tone.

'Or what?' said Chad, still not deterred by the sight of his friend lying on the floor with blood trickling out from his nose.

'Or I'll…' but the man was interrupted by the sound of ringing. It was coming from his pocket. 'Aww man, not now.'

He reached into pocket and pulled out a pair of handcuffs. In a swift movement, he grabbed Chad and cuffed him to the tap. From his other pocket, he pulled out his phone and answered it.

'Hello… oh hi mum… my voice? … oh, uh, I have a sore throat … yeah,

I will… okay, I'll pick some up and drop them off later … okay, mum I've got to go now … no, I don't care about the woman next door, look I've got to go … okay, bye mum … yes, I… I love you too … bye.'

The man pocketed his phone and turned back to Chad, who had just been looking on in bemusement at the strangely ordinary phone call.

'Okay, so where were we?' the man asked.

'Well, you'd just punched my friend and then you cuffed me to this tap,' said Chad, as he returned to his worried state, as if they'd been rehearsing a play and briefly stopped for a drink.

'Oh yeah. Right, now are you going to wash your hands, or are we going to have to do this the hard way?'

Chad gulped. 'What's the hard way?'

'I cut off your hands and wash them myself.'

'Ha, with what?' asked Chad with a slightly nervous laugh.

The man pulled back his cape slowly to reveal what was clipped to the left side of his belt.

'A pack of wet wipes?' asked a confused Chad.

'Huh? Oh, sorry. New belt,' said Cap. He pulled back the cape on the other side to reveal a large pair of secateurs attached to his belt.

Chad let out a little squeal. 'I'll wash them! I'll wash them!'

He fumbled around and managed to turn on the tap that his wrist was still cuffed to. He rinsed his hands under the water, smiling nervously at the man, looking desperately for approval.

'With soap,' said the masked man sternly. 'All over.'

Chad nodded frantically. 'Of course,' he said, as he covered his hands in a ridiculous amount of soap and washed them as thoroughly as he could.

'Good. Now make sure you do that every time you finish in the toilet,' he said, talking as if Chad were a young schoolboy learning for the first time.

'I will, I promise,' said Chad, nodding furiously. 'C-can I go now?'

The toilet roll-covered stranger nodded his toilet paper-covered head and uncuffed Chad, who promptly ran out of the toilets. The masked man heard a groan and looked down at the floor, where the other young teen was still lying clutching his nose.

'Hey! You forgot your…' he called after Chad, but there was no way he'd hear him now. He just shrugged and muttered, 'Ah forget it.'

He pulled the toilet paper back over his mouth and headed for the door. As he was leaving, the kid on the floor sat up.

'Uh mister… who are you?' the boy asked.

'Irf cupfhuhn cruuhm,' mumbled the man.

'Huh?' he replied.

The man pulled the toilet roll away from his mouth and repeated, 'I'm Captain Clean.'

♦♦

Six years and a few weeks later.

It was early and so was he. Martin Daley paced the corridor, running through his presentation one last time. Today was the day he finally gave his pitch to the head of product development at LoTech, Filtham's largest technology company – "why settle for high tech when you can have LoTech" as their advert proudly boasted. Their products were expensive and solved problems that nobody knew even existed until LoTech told them they did. If you didn't have the latest LoTech computer, TV or stereo system, you were a nobody. Or at least that's what their adverts with the sexy young couples liked to make you believe.

Martin was a short man in his forties, and everything about him was round. His rotund belly, which had long since given in to his love of cake; his balding head, which certain tribes might have rubbed for good luck; and his bulbous nose that made it look like he was holding in a dozen sneezes. Martin had been working on his presentation for weeks and he knew that, if he pulled it off, he would get the promotion he so desperately wanted and felt he deserved. He checked his watch. 8:54am. He still had six minutes until the meeting. As he leaned against the wall and rehearsed his pitch for the 17th time that morning, a familiar face came around the corner. Victor Timm, his colleague and arch-nemesis. It was a bold term to describe someone, but Martin felt it applied. Victor was taller, slimmer and had more hair than Martin, but he didn't have a 10% discount at the local bakery like Martin did – he loved the tarts in that bakery, and liked their cakes too. He had joined the company at the same time as Martin and it hadn't been long before a rivalry was born. He was the sort that did very little and showed no respect, but somehow managed to succeed at everything. He won all his pitches, got all the bonuses and copped off with all the new girls at the Christmas party. And now he was trying to take Martin's promotion from him too.

'Oh, you're going for the job too?' said Victor, pretending like he hadn't found out a week before from Janet from HR while they were making out in the stationery cupboard.

'Yes,' said Martin, clutching his folder a little tighter but still trying to appear unphased.

'Well, good luck I guess,' he said with a smirk. 'You're gonna need it.'

'Damn straight I am!' said Martin in a strangely confident tone.

Victor was interviewing after Martin, so he went into the toilet to relieve himself first. After he'd done his business, he sauntered over to the taps. Rather than wash his hands, though, he checked himself out in the mirror and adjusted some individual strands of hair that were covered in a thick layer of gel. Had he not been so focussed on admiring his perfectly combed hair, he would've heard the faint crackle as a flaky crust started to grow at a rapid pace around the taps.

The counter began to shake a little, and cracks started forming, gradually growing out from the sink along the worktop. Victor continued to be oblivious to what was going on below him, far too interested in his own reflection to pay anything else in the world any attention. He smiled at himself in the mirror and gave a cheeky wink. At the precise moment the mirror caught his wink, the sink below him suddenly gave way, collapsing in on itself and pulling the taps down with it into the hole below.

The area in front of him exploded with jets of water, splashing up like someone on the ceiling was having a shower, and soaking the floor beneath him. Victor jumped back and let out a high-pitched scream. He panicked and made a run for the door, but the wet floor made him stumble and the collapsing ground around him pulled him down. He felt some kind of hand rise up and grab his leg, surprisingly light to the touch, but making a crunching sound as it gripped him. He screamed and shouted, crying out for help with high pitched squeals that evaporated any coolness he had.

Outside, Martin became alerted to the tumultuous fracas coming from inside the toilets. He wasn't usually one to put himself in any kind of danger, but knowing who was inside, he felt he had to at least check it out, if only to have something to hold over Victor later. He tried to open the door, but something was jamming it from the inside. He pushed and kicked it with all his strength – which wasn't much – and eventually the door gave way, pushing aside the rubble that was blocking its path.

Martin peered in just in time to see a grotesque, grainy claw pull Victor down into the hole where the sink had been. He stood aghast as Victor's screams slowly faded away. Martin stumbled backwards out of the toilets and fell into the corridor. He was terrified by what he'd seen and didn't know what to do.

At that moment, the meeting room door opened and one of the senior members of staff came out to get him.

'We're ready for you Martin,' said the interviewer.

'Wh... but... in the... Vic... and the...' he stuttered, still in shock.

'It's okay, there's nothing to worry about,' the man said, taking Martin's arm and guiding him into the boardroom. 'Everyone gets nervous before an interview.'

He led Martin inside and closed the door behind them.

♦ ♦

Filtham Community Centre was a stone's throw away from the city centre – if the person throwing the stone was an Olympic javelin champion that had been exposed to radiation and gained super strength. It was a place where the people of the community could gather and enjoy themselves and revel in exercise for both the body and brain. The first and third floors were home to regular activities for children, the elderly and anyone else who didn't fall into either of those two categories. From coffee mornings and book clubs to martial arts and pottery, the community centre offered a little slice of joy and culture to the city. The second floor, however, was off limits to the public. It was said to be space that politicians and very important businesspeople used for private meetings, but this was merely a cover for something far more interesting.

In a small office on the second floor, Clifford Cane was sat at his desk, reading a book entitled "Microbial Choreography: Biofilm Formation and Communication in Bacterial Colonies" by the author I.M. Boring. Clifford was a middle-aged man, with short hair and no other real distinctive features. He was a tall and well-built, muscular but still with a bit of a 'dad bod'. Overall, his physical appearance was extraordinarily ordinary. Suddenly, a knock on the door disturbed the silence. A woman poked her head around the door. She was dressed smartly, with an outfit accentuated with purple skirt and boots, and matching gloves. Her top was white though, because dressing all in purple would have made her look like a walking aubergine. She wore a belt with several small spray bottles and plastic sample tubes attached to it, finished with a buckle in the shape of a circle with a water droplet over it. She had long brown hair and a kind face that had clearly been worn down by years of stressful work and frown lines on her forehead that were reserved for her boss.

'We've got another one Cliff,' she said.

Clifford looked up excitedly, happy for some action after a quiet few days. 'Where?' he asked.

'The LoTech building,' she told him. 'The police report says he witnessed a man disappear down a sink.'

'Is he still there?'

'No, he disappeared down a sink.'

'I mean the witness.'

'No, the police sent him home and passed his number on to a local psychiatrist.'

'Great, I'll pay him a visit.'

'The psychiatrist?'

'No, the sink man,' he grumbled.

'Ah, shame,' she muttered. 'I thought for a minute there you might get some help.'

'I don't need help,' said Clifford, standing up. 'I need answers. And tea, but that can wait.'

Clifford walked over to a machine on the wall and pushed a button on it. A small roll of what looked like toilet paper popped dropped down onto a little tray at the bottom. He took the roll and started wrapping the paper around the top half of his head.

You see, Clifford was better known as Captain Clean – or Cap to his friends, who were mainly his colleagues as he didn't have the time (or social skills) for friends. Captain Clean was the leader of the Sanitary Squad, a group of "grime fighting heroes", set up and funded by the council, that dealt mainly with sanitation themed crimes. For some reason, there seemed to be a lot of sanitation themed crimes going on in the city. Some people suspected it may have been in direct response to the Sanitary Squad forming, but nobody really said anything, as very little else happened in the city and it was something exciting to watch on the news instead of news stories about annoying celebrities cheating on each other with even more annoying celebrities.

The woman who had brought the news was Dr Jean Wilkes – known in the squad as HyJean – and she was the brains behind the group. She was gifted when it came to technology, science and pretty much anything that she put her brilliant mind to. She was a competent fighter, but her strength lay more in being a strong strategic thinker, often avoiding fights through more clever means. With several degrees and a wealth of experience working at some of the top scientific research institutes, she was arguably overqualified for the squad, but that didn't stop her. Since she'd mentioned in her interview that she owned a computer, she was also put in charge of monitoring the criminal activity in the city using a series of computers that lined one of the walls in the base – actually just one computer with several cheap monitors to make it look a bit more impressive. She was also frequently bombarded with questions about phones not working or broken coffee machines, because that's what happens when you use a computer for work, everyone thinks you're a technician who can fix any technical fault.

Like most of the squad's equipment, HyJean had developed the captain's toilet paper mask, making it out of a special material so that it was extra durable and waterproof. She'd also advised him to remove the bottom half so that he could be heard more clearly – a decision which she often regretted.

The captain was dressed in his usual blue shirt with blue jeans and yellow boots. He would've liked a professional uniform for his squad, but their budget from the council only allowed them the luxury of a few accessories to spice up their everyday clothes. His included a yellow cape made of a special stain-resistant waterproof micro-fibre cloth, leather marigold gloves and a belt that had a buckle with a water droplet insignia on it that matched HyJean's. This was the squad's logo, although the design was less by choice and more because he'd seen the belt buckles going cheap on a plumber's stall at a car boot sale and bought a load of them.

He then moved over to a row of sticks that were hung on the wall. Each had a different appendage on the end, including a toilet brush, a pair of plungers and a short mop. They looked like ordinary cleaning tools, but again, HyJean had modified them to make them infinitely more useful. The toilet brush had metal bristles that were very painful when smashed against your face – as the captain had accidentally found out the first time he used it – the plungers had enough suction for someone to easily climb a wall, and the mop could spin at an alarming speed that was enough to lift someone a few inches off the floor – something that rarely came in useful. Today, Captain Clean opted for the toilet brush, which he retracted and clipped to his belt. He probably wouldn't need it, but it made him feel safe and he thought it made him look cool. He thought wrongly. Nobody wearing yellow leather marigolds with toilet wrapped around their heads looks cool.

'What else do we know?' he asked as he made his way out of his office. 'What's their security like? Could someone have broken in?'

'I doubt it. Their security is top notch, as you'd expect,' she replied. 'Windows and doors are all alarmed, scanners at all entrances, and all their best tech is chipped so it can't leave the building without the boss's say so. Something that could do this wouldn't be easy to sneak in.'

'Interesting,' said the captain. 'You got the address?'

'Sort of,' she replied, handing him a small note. 'I've found out what street he lives on, but not which number. I'm afraid you'll have to do this one the old-fashioned way.'

'Thanks,' the captain sighed. 'While I'm out, see what else you can find in the media that might be of some use.'

On the way out, the captain passed a small office with an older, grey-haired woman sat inside, tapping at a computer that she barely knew how to use. Her desk piled high with papers, hiding the small plant that was so desperately craving sunlight. The woman was Mary Goldman, the squad's secretary in charge of admin. Being a council-funded operation, there was often a lot of paperwork (invoices for damages, purchase orders for new equipment, expenses, etc.) so Clifford had hired Mary to take care of it all.

'Can you cancel my 1 o'clock lunch appointment please Mary, I'm going out.'

'You haven't got a 1 o'clock lunch appointment,' she replied, turning to him and pressing her glasses back up the bridge of her nose.

'Really?' asked a bemused captain, 'I thought I did?'

'I cancelled it when I saw Jean going into your office.'

'You're far too good Mary.'

'I know,' Mary grinned as the captain left.

💧 💧

Captain Clean stood at the top of Witnessal Street and wondered which side to start on. The police would have already visited Mr Daley, because they knew where everyone lived – they were nosey like that. The captain had asked for access to their databases several times, but apparently giving out personal data to strange people who run around in silly outfits wasn't something the commissioner was very keen to do. HyJean had suggested trying to hack their system to get the data, but the captain was insistent that they shouldn't do that as it was "probably illegal".

'Might as well start with number one,' Captain Clean said. He marched up to the first door on the left side of the road and knocked on it. While he waited, the captain noticed that the door knocker was quite dirty, so he pulled a cloth out from a little compartment on his belt and gave it a quick wipe. After a short wait, the door opened to reveal a rather jittery man who appeared to be 50 years old, although he'd actually been wearing the 50th birthday badge for over 2 years now. The resident of the house was surprised to find a strange-looking man polishing his door knocker.

'Oh, hello,' said Captain Clean, suddenly spotting the man at the door and hiding his cloth. 'Are you Martin?'

'No, I'm Brian,' replied Brian in a nervous tremor. 'Why? Who sent you? Is this to do with the courgettes again?'

'No, no. I'm with the council,' he explained, not mentioning the squad as this would likely frighten the man even more. 'I'm looking for a Mr Martin Daley. I don't suppose you know where he lives do you?'

'I don't know anything!' shouted the nervous Brian before slamming the door in the captain's face.

Cap made a little note in his notebook: 1 Witnessal Street, suspicious nutter.

He carried on down to 3 Witnessal Street and once again knocked on the door. This time a little girl, no more than 6 years old, opened the door.

'Hello little girl, does anybody called Martin live here?' he asked, not even making his voice sound friendlier, just talking to her like an adult.

'I'm not supposed to talk to strangers,' she replied, talking to him like he was an idiot.

'I'm not a stranger,' he said. 'I'm Captain Clean and I'm –'

'Your outfit is pretty strange,' she interrupted.

'No it's not, I'm a superhero.'

'Really? Can you fly?'

'Well… not per se.'

'What does that mean?'

'It's a fancy way of saying no.'

'Oh. Can you shoot lasers from your eyes?'

'No.'

'Can you run faster than a speeding bullet?'

'I don't think so, but I've never really tried.'

'So, what powers do you have?'

'Um… a thirst for justice and a brown belt in karate, ju jitsu and kick boxing.'

'My brother's got a black belt in karate.'

'Alright kid, it's not a competition.'

At this point, the girl's mother came to the door to see who her daughter had been talking to. She was not exactly pleased to see it was a man whose face was wrapped in toilet paper.

'Ah, hello madam,' said Captain Clean, 'I was just speaking to your daughter.'

'About what?' asked the worried mother, 'Who are you?'

'It's alright mum, I've got it,' said the girl. 'We don't know anyone called Martin, now clear off you dirty old perv!'

And with that the girl slammed the door in his face.

Captain Clean had to admit that he wasn't off to a great start, and his next few attempts didn't go too well either. But eventually, after knocking on 32 doors on the left side of the street, he did find someone who knew where Martin lived. As it transpired, Martin lived at number 2 Witnessal Street – the first house on the right side of the street. Oh, how the captain cursed when he found that out.

💧💧

Martin was surprised to see a man who looked like he'd just come from a fancy-dress party standing on his doorstep. It hadn't been the first time, though. A few months prior, he'd opened the door to find a man dressed as a priest outside. One of the local lads had been to a fancy-dress party, gotten very drunk, become convinced he was a real priest and started knocking on doors asking if anyone needed him to perform an exorcism. Only one person did, and it went surprisingly well.

'Can I help you?' Martin asked as he looked the grime fighter up and down.

'Are you Martin Daley?' asked Captain Clean.

'Yes,' Martin replied.

'Thank god for that,' he sighed. 'I'm here to talk about your hand.'

'My hand?' Martin asked with a bemused look, instinctively feeling his left hand with his right as if it were about to fall off.

'Yes, the hand you saw snatch the guy in the toilets at work,' the captain explained. 'May I come in?'

'I… I suppose so,' Martin nodded, still rubbing his left hand just to be sure.

He invited the captain into his living room and went off to make him a cup of tea. The costumed hero sat on the sofa, looking somewhat out of place in the council house living room trying to avoid the small dog on the sofa next to him that was sniffing his gloves. He'd always held the view that pets – and animals in general – were highly unsanitary and not to be trusted. After a few minutes, Martin returned with the tea and a plate of biscuits. The captain would neither drink the tea nor eat the biscuits, as he could not be certain how clean Martin's kitchen was.

'Get off the sofa, you daft bugger,' Martin said as he entered the room.

'Oh, sorry' said the captain, quickly standing up.

'Not you, the dog,' Martin clarified.

Martin moved the dog away from the captain and sent him off to play in the garden. The captain sat back down and began his investigation.

'How are you feeling, Mr Daley?' he asked.

'I'm not too bad, thanks,' Martin said cheerily. 'How are you?'

'I'm hungry, Mr Daley,' the captain replied.

'Oh, would you like some biscuits?' he replied, moving to pick up the plate.

'No, Mr Daley,' said the captain, now leaning in more seriously. 'I'm hungry for the truth.'

'Oooh,' said Martin, who had been drawn into the theatrical nature of the costumed man's demeanour. 'If you don't mind me asking, who are you exactly? You're not a Jehovah's Witness are you?'

'My name is Captain Clean. I'm a grime fighter with a group called the Sanitary Squad – we investigate this sort of phemon… phemomom… phenonon… strange goings on,' he explained. So, what can you tell me about the victim?'

'Victor Timm? Oh, he's a smarmy git,' said Martin in a very matter of fact manner that clearly conveyed his dislike for the man. 'Thinks he's god's gift to women, always spends ages checking himself out in any mirror he's nearby. And he keeps using my stapler without asking!'

'Okay, thank you, but I meant more his physical appearance,' the captain clarified.

'Oh, well he's taller than me, slimmer than me, more smartly dressed than me,' he said with an air of contempt. 'And his hair's gelled back so slick you'd think an army of snails had slid over his head.'

'Very well,' said the captain, recognising that he wasn't going to get an unbiased opinion of the man. 'Tell me about what happened to Mr Timm when he went into the toilets.'

'Well,' said Martin, clearing his throat and sitting back to tell the story that he'd told police and journalists many times already. 'He went in to go for a slash and it was quite normal for about a minute, just the usual sounds you know.'

Martin paused and raised his eyebrows. The captain nodded to show that he was well acquainted with the sounds men usually make when they go to the toilet.

'Did he wash his hands while he was in there?' asked the captain.

'I don't think so, I didn't hear the tap running. I was listening in you see, trying to hear him practice his pitch – not that he did, he's too confident for stuff like that. Anyway, I just heard this crashing and screaming,' Martin continued, 'I went inside to have a look, and the sinks had been destroyed and he was being pulled down into a hole.'

'Was there anyone in the toilets before your colleague entered?'

'Not that I know of.'

'Did you see what the hand looked like?'

'Yes.'

There was a slight pause and the Captain sighed, 'Would you care to tell me?'

'Oh, sorry. Well, it was horrible. There were four fingers and a thumb, like a human hand, you know, but they were long and thin – like talons they were. And the skin was a dirty grey, and crusty, with dark yellow flaky scales. It was like something out of them alien films.'

'I doubt this is an alien invasion.'

'But that's what they always say, in the films, right before an alien invasion.'

'This isn't a film Mr Daley, it's real life.'

'They say that as well,' said Martin, getting more and more worked up.

'Mr Daley, there's nothing to worry about,' said the captain, trying to calm him down.

'That's always their last words right before they're killed!' He stood up and started pacing around, jittery at the thought of an impending alien invasion.

The captain picked up his cup of tea and flung its contents in Martin's face.

'Mr Daley, calm down!'

'Sorry, I'm a bit nervy when it comes to aliens,' he explained as he sat down. He wiped his tea-soaked face with a biscuit and then ate it. 'I was attacked by someone in an ET costume out trick or treating when I was young. Never liked them since.'

The captain continued to ask a few more questions, making notes as he did, then sat in thought for a moment. Martin drummed his fingers on the chair, a little unsure what was happening and whether to interrupt the captain's musings to offer him more tea.

'One last question Mr Daley, has there been any other unusual activity in the building recently?'

'I don't think so. I mean, the printer kept jamming last Tuesday, but I don't think that's got anything to do with it.'

'No, I don't think so either,' the captain said as he stood up to leave. 'Thank you, that's all for now.'

'Are you sure you wouldn't like a biscuit?' asked Martin.

'Give mine to the dog,' the captain replied.

'But he doesn't like rich tea.'

'Then he will enjoy it just as much as I would.'

💧💧

When Captain Clean arrived back at the base, he was greeted by Sergeant Suds; a man several years older than the captain, but much more muscular. He was mostly bald, and wore a military green outfit of cargo pants, vest and heavy black boots. Mick Goldman, as he was known outside of work, was married to Mary, but had joined the squad a few months before her. He had originally signed up to the army, but a mistake on his form meant he'd signed up to be a cleaner rather than a soldier. He spent a few years there, cleaning the barracks and longing for more action. This was also where he'd earned the nickname Sergeant Suds from the soldiers who he'd become friends with. When he left the army, he joined the squad and used the skills he'd learned in the army to help fight grime. HyJean had even created him a special gun that fired soap at various consistencies, allowing him to fire a watery slime if he needed to slip someone up, or a thick, sticky ooze if he wanted to trap someone.

Suds had been out in the morning, dealing with a rather deranged man, who had branded himself the Dust Devil, that had been running around the city with a homemade gun that created mini tornados.

'How did you get on?' asked Captain Clean.

'Wasn't too much trouble. I was able to disrupt the airflow with my soap and after that it was just a case of punching him real hard,' he replied as he removed his fake grey goatee beard, which he wore partly as a disguise and partly because he'd never been able to grow an actual beard and liked how he looked with the fake facial hair.

'Excellent work, although I do wish you'd tone down the violence a little; it's not great for our image,' the captain replied. As he looked up, he noticed a small trail of soil on the floor that Suds had left.

'Mick! Your boots,' he said, jumping up and running over to the sergeant. He pushed him against the wall and bent down, tugging furiously at the black, heavy boots.

'Hey! What are you doing?' Suds asked as he tried to retain his balance.

'You've got dirt on them!' the captain replied as though he were alerting him to an oncoming tornado.

'It's fine, it's just a bit of soil is all,' Suds replied, pushing the captain off him and taking his own boots off. 'Relax will you, a bit of soil isn't going to kill anyone.'

'You never know,' the captain replied. 'Do you know how many soil-related deaths there are every year?'

'No. Do you?' Suds replied, raising an eyebrow. He knew the captain wouldn't know the answer. He never did. He would often try to hype things up and threaten people with stats but rarely knew the answers himself. And if he did, his memory was so bad that he'd likely forget them anyway.

'That's beside the point,' said the captain, with his usual deflection. 'Anyway, clear up that mess and ask Jean to spray your boots later. I've told you before, if you buy new shoes, they need to be sprayed.'

The spray in question was a special concoction that HyJean had invented that made the soles of their footwear completely stain resistant, meaning that any water, mud or the other kind of unpleasant animal-related substance people sometimes step in would simply slide off. It didn't keep them one hundred percent clean, but it was sufficient enough to keep the floors of the base dirt-free to Captain Clean's satisfactory standard.

While Suds wandered off in his socks to get the dustpan and brush, the captain headed over to the furthest wall of the base where HyJean was sat at a set of computers. She had clearly had a busy afternoon, as there were four mugs of coffee on her desk. Her colleagues were able to measure how busy or stressed HyJean was by how many mugs were on her desk and how neatly or randomly they were arranged. A couple of mugs in a neat row was a fairly quiet morning, but half a dozen mugs spread around the desk was a hectic one.

'What did he say?' HyJean asked the captain without even looking around.

'Not a lot, pretty much what was in the report,' he replied, before recounting their conversation to HyJean. 'Though I did find it odd that he said the hand was crusty and flaky, like an alien hand.'

'Interesting,' she said, and it was interesting enough for her to look around this time. 'I wonder what it could be. Did he say what colour?'

'He said a dirty grey – although all grey is dirty to me – with yellow flakes or scales,' said the captain.

'Interesting twice over,' said HyJean, turning back to the computers. 'Anyway, I've got a few things to show you.'

The captain stood watching as HyJean rolled around on her swivel chair presenting her findings.

'There's been a few reports of toilets being trashed and they all correlate with people going missing. The victims are generally people in high powered jobs in specific industries, such as engineering and mechanics, so my guess is this person's building something and is kidnapping people with expertise.'

She rolled the chair over to the next computer and continued.

'This isn't the first time it's happened at LoTech, but the first time it was kept hush, with the police writing it off as an act of vandalism.'

She rolled over to another computer at the other end of the desk, like she was a dancer gliding across the floor and stopping with grace.

'There have also been several tweets with people complaining about strange noises coming from underground, but the council have checked the sewers and there's nothing odd down there.'

'Interesting,' said the captain. 'Jean, I think we should start by checking out the LoTech building, see what we can find.'

'Okay, but can we go after lunch? I'm starving,' asked HyJean.

The captain agreed. He'd not eaten either and there was even the tiniest part of him that was slightly regretting not taking one of Martin Daley's biscuits, so he sent Mary to the local café to get some sandwiches for the rest of the squad while he had one he'd prepared at home. Captain Clean rarely ate food he hadn't prepared himself, as he didn't trust the hygiene levels of kitchens he couldn't see, and it had become embarrassing being repeatedly thrown out of restaurants for insisting on inspecting the kitchens.

♦ ♦

With their bellies full, Captain Clean and HyJean now stood outside the LoTech building. The entrance was blocked off, with police cars, policemen and intrigued people who were not affiliated with the police all looking on at the crime scene through mobile phone screens, hoping to catch a bit of gossip to tell their friends later. It's a sad fact that with the rise of technology, people's reactions to situations have gone from concern for the wellbeing and safety of others to concern for how many views their footage of it will get on social media. And while victims may be immortalised on film, this does not provide them any comfort. Unless their situation is embarrassing and they get hold of the video and send it off to a TV show that shows clips of people in funny situations, in which case they could earn a bit of money.

'How are we going to get in?' asked HyJean.

'Is there a back entrance?' asked the captain.

'I don't know, I've never been here before.'

'Then where do you buy all our equipment?'

'From a shop, like any normal person.'

'Fine, then I'll need you to create some sort of distraction so I can sneak in.'

'Hold on, why are you going in?' asked HyJean, sounding a bit cheesed off.

'To investigate,' explained the captain.

'No offence, but as the resident scientist, I think I'd be better off going in,' she replied. 'I can analyse the wreckage and take any samples I might need.'

'Offence taken, and I'm still going in,' said the captain firmly. 'Now help me create a distraction.'

HyJean thought for a moment and then had an idea.

'Okay, take your mask and cape off and go into the crowd,' she told him. 'Make out like you've spotted something and start shouting to get people's attention. Then I'll jump out and pretend to fight it off, while you slip into the building.'

'Good idea,' said the captain, taking off his cape and mask sticking them under his shirt, making it look like he had a large pot belly. 'I think I can do that. I did go to RADA.'

'Really?' asked HyJean.

'Yeah, a few years ago, but it was shut when I got there.'

Captain Clean slipped into the crowd and began his theatrics. He pointed in the opposite direction down the road and started shouting. 'Oh my goodness, look! There is a giant robot heading this way! Somebody stop it!'

As he'd hoped, everybody turned to see where the imaginary giant robot was. Not-as-he'd-hoped, HyJean then snuck inside the building, leaving a desperate Captain Clean to try and explain to disgruntled onlookers why there was no giant robot down the street.

'Idiot,' HyJean muttered as she entered the building and swiftly made her way up to the 6th floor, where she'd read the incident had happened. Rather than try to sneak around and keep hidden, she just confidently walked straight to the toilets, where she saw a familiar face. At the door was a short, portly police officer with a scraggly ginger beard.

'Officer Down!' called out HyJean.

'What? No! Where?' the police officer cried, jumping to the floor and pulling out his gun.

'Put the gun down, Sid, I'm talking to you,' HyJean said with a roll of her eyes. She offered a hand to help him up. 'Come on, get up.'

'Oh, sorry,' said Officer Down. He chuckled as he stood back up and put his gun away. 'Easy mistake. Still, I'm sure I'll get used to it once I've been in the job a while.'

'You've been saying that for the past 2 years.'

'Oh? Has it been that long? Well, doesn't time cry... uh, fly.'

Officer Sidney Down wasn't the best that Filtham City Police Department had to offer – ranking somewhere just above the water cooler – but somehow, he'd managed to keep his job on the force long enough to be in charge of a walkie talkie. He was a nervous man and was often prone to getting his words mixed up, much to the amusement of the other officers.

'Hm, yes,' she said, shrugging off his remark. 'Anyway, I'm here to inspect the crime scene.'

'But you can't, nobody's allowed in. Chief's orders,' he explained, puffing his chest out a little to seem important.

'He's given me clearance, that's why I'm up here,' HyJean said coolly. 'Ask him yourself if you don't believe me.'

'Okay. Sorry love, nothing personal, just more than my job's worth,' he said as he pulled out a pair of handcuffs and put them to his ear. 'Oops, wrong socket… uh, pocket.'

He chuckled as he put the handcuffs back and pulled out his walkie talkie from the other pocket, but as he switched it on, a prepared HyJean discretely flipped a switch on a nifty little device in her pocket that scrambled the signal to his walkie talkie.

'I can't get hold of him, I'll have to go down and ask him,' said the policeman. 'Just wait here until I get back. And don't touch any elephants… uh, evidence.'

Once he'd left to find his boss, HyJean, ignoring the officer's orders, continued into the toilets. Her footsteps squelched and crunch as she made her way across the water and rubble that covered the floor.

'Thanks officer,' she said as she entered the room, fooling the policemen inside into thinking she'd been given permission. 'Alright then lads, let's take a look.'

Unsure what to do in the presence of a costumed lady, one of the policemen saluted, but the other one nudged him and told him to put his hand down. HyJean crouched down and inspected the great hole. She noted that, unusually, there were two sets of pipes leading up, one small pipe and another that was considerably wider than the other – almost big enough to fit a small human. She shone her light down and took a closer look at the larger pipe, which was lined with the remnants of a dirty yellow, crusty substance.

'That looks like… limescale,' she muttered to herself as she out a small scalpel and chipped off a bit into a little plastic bag. 'I wonder how that got there.'

'The plumber was surprised by that too,' said one of the policemen.

'Hm?' asked HyJean.

'They had a plumber out here to take a look,' he explained. 'And he said there shouldn't be any limescale in the pipes because they're not connected to the main water supply.'

'He didn't know what it was connected to,' added his colleague. 'We reckon there's a monster in the sewers.'

'Like a mutant snake, slithering up to grab people,' said the other, clearly enjoying theorising what was down there.

'If it was connected to the sewers, it'd be part of the sewage pipework, by the toilets,' HyJean pointed out. 'So why build extra pipes next to the water supply pipes?'

As the two men contemplated their theories with this new information, HyJean heard a faint but familiar voice coming down the corridor.

'I think that's enough for now,' she said, gathering her things and quickly exiting the toilets, running around the corner at the opposite end of the corridor to avoid being seen by the approaching policeman, who had now learnt that she didn't have permission to enter the scene at all.

'Where is she?' asked Officer Down.

'Who?' asked one of the policemen in the toilets.

'The Sanitary Squad woman who was just in here,' said Officer Down in an exasperated tone that people usually used with him.

'Oh, she's gone,' said the policeman.

'I think she got everything she needed though,' added the other policeman.

'You idiots, she wasn't supposed to be in here,' explained Officer Down.

'Really?' said the first policeman. 'But she seemed so nice.'

'Look, none of you mention this to the beef… uh, the chief,' said Officer Down. 'If he asks, we got rid of her straight away. Okay?'

The two policemen agreed to keep it quiet and went back to staring at the hole, pretending they knew what they were doing, when in actuality they were just passing time until they could go back down and declare their findings to be inconclusive.

HyJean, meanwhile, had made it to a stairwell and found a board that showed what was on each floor of the building. Scanning it, she saw that the CEO's office was on the next floor up. She doubted that he'd be there now, but it was still worth a look around. She climbed the stairs and made her way to the office. The lights were off in the corridor and there was an air of silence, making it feel creepy and dramatic. Things always seem creepier in the dark, even when you're in a familiar place. Our minds conjure up images of murderers jumping out on us with knives or ghosts watching us, even though the doors are locked and ghosts are just images projected by our brain to try and fill in missing information in the presence of something inexplicable. Still, HyJean found herself focusing on the one spec of light bleeding out from the bottom of a door at the end of the corridor. As she got closer, she crept slower, listening to the faint sobbing noises coming from inside the room. This made her feel a little safer, as knife-wielding murders and ghosts don't usually spend their time crying in locked rooms. Although, if films are to be believed, ghosts often sit around crying – and why shouldn't they, they're dead. The sign on the door read "Peter Lotech, CEO" so she knew she was in the right place. The door was slightly ajar, so she tentatively pushed it open and entered.

'Are you okay?' she asked softly.

This startled the crying man, who jumped in his chair and knocked over the glass of water he'd been nursing. He stumbled to his feet with a look that was more nervous than angry. 'Who are you? How did you get in here? What do you want?'

'My name is HyJean and I'm here to help,' she said calmly, taking out a cloth from her utility belt and cleaning up the spilled water, as if this somehow proved that she was not a threat. Peter watched, a little confused, as she stood the glass up and put her surprisingly absorbent cloth away.

'You're not with the police?' the CEO asked.

'It's that obvious?' she said with a slight chuckle. 'No, I'm with the Sanitary Squad. We're a group of grime fighters, funded by the government, and we've been asked to look into this matter by one of your employees, Martin Daley. It's kind of our speciality.'

Peter slumped down into his chair, seemingly already defeated and not in a mood to protest HyJean's presence. 'Well, I guess it doesn't matter now, the whole city seems to know what's going on this time,' he sighed. 'I just don't know what to do. An employee goes missing and nobody's got the foggiest idea how it happened, except for one guy who keeps rambling on about alien hands. I've had to shut the building down and the staff are all terrified. This could be the end of us.'

'Mr Lotech, you said "this time",' asked HyJean. 'This has happened before, hasn't it?'

'What? No,' said Peter, looking more nervous than ever. 'No, I just… I meant this time as in this time of day.'

'Look, Mr Lotech, if this has happened before, I need to know,' said HyJean, clearly not buying his ridiculous story. 'It could help us figure out what's going on and prevent it happening again.'

'But… I…' he stuttered, before sighing heavily once again. 'You said you're not with the police?'

'No, but you can trust me,' said HyJean. 'We won't tell anyone anything. That's not why we're here.'

'Fine, then yes, it happened before,' said the CEO, taking out a bottle of whiskey and pouring himself some. He offered it to HyJean, but she refused. 'A few weeks back, the same thing happened. We had some issues with the water, so it was turned off. Nobody was supposed to be using the facilities on site, but a woman went into one of the toilets and was kidnapped in the same way. Since we were already doing maintenance on the toilets, we closed it off until it was repaired and the police said they'd look into it. They haven't come back to us with anything and they just put her down as a missing person.'

'I see,' said HyJean, pausing to take in the whole story, piecing it together in her mind. 'So, a woman goes missing and you just covered it up?'

'I didn't… what could I do?' said Peter with a pitiful look of shame on his face. 'I didn't want to scare my employees. I mean how do you explain that someone went into a toilet and disappeared?'

'That's precisely what I'm going to try and work out,' said HyJean, making her way over to the door. She gave him one final look, but this time it wasn't of compassion or friendliness; it was a look of disgust. 'And let's just hope your two employees are still alive.'

♦ ♦

As HyJean and Captain Clean arrived back at the base, they were greeted by Mary, who had news. In this respect, she was a bit like a newsreader. Although in every other respect, she wasn't. She had never been on television, rarely wore a suit and was not reading the news she had off an autocue. Unlike newsreaders, she was able to remember the news she had. So, in this respect, she was better than a newsreader.

'Captain, I'm glad you're back. I've just had a call from a Dr Scope at the hospital,' she informed them. 'She's asked if you can go see her urgently. They've had a patient in with some very unusual symptoms that she thinks you might be able to advise on.'

'Okay,' said the captain. 'Jean, you'd best come too. You're much better at this sort of stuff.'

'What, talking to women?' came a voice from behind.

The voice belonged to Will Armitage, better known as Flush. He's the final member of the Sanitary Squad and has not featured until now because he was busy – not busy fighting grime, but rather doing another job entirely. You see, Flush was only a part time hero, as he also had another part-time job, though none of the squad knew what it was he did. When he joined the squad, he specifically requested that his other job be kept separate and refused to share any details about it, having seen in films what happens when superheroes and their daytime jobs collided. Captain Clean reluctantly agreed, though would still randomly ask him questions about it from time to time to try and catch him out. Flush was a good few years younger than most of the squad and saw himself as the cool one of the group. He wore a trendier outfit that consisted of dark teal trousers, matching teal sneakers and a white polo shirt with a teal collar, topped off with a mask and a spiky blonde wig that covered his naturally brown hair – designed to protect his identity that little bit more. His weapon of choice was an extendable whip that had been fashioned to look like an old toilet chain.

'Ah Will, just in time,' said the captain. 'We've got a little trip we need you to go on.'

'Ooh nice, where am I going today?' he said, rubbing his hands together with an excited smile. He was mainly doing this sarcastically, as their excursions were rarely nice places like a pool or a bar, but he still lived in hope.

'The library,' grinned the captain.

Flush's face fell. 'The library?'

'Yes, it's a place where they store books,' said HyJean.

'I know what a library is!' he groaned. 'I checked a book out a few weeks ago as it happens.'

'How's that going by the way?' asked Suds. 'Have you found Wally yet?'

'Shut up! I read proper books I do. Christopher Dickens, T.S. Lewis.'

'A.A. Milne?' suggested HyJean.

'Ah no, that's a trick one!' said Flush. 'He's not an author. He's the guy who invented the car breakdown service.'

'Anyway!' interrupted the captain. 'I need you to go to the library and find the original plans for the LoTech building. HyJean found out they have two sets of pipework and nobody there seems to know why. If we can find out what the second pipe is doing there and where it leads, we might have a clue as to where to find our kidnapper.'

'Mick, you'd better go with him,' said HyJean, adding with a grin, 'in case there's any long words to read.'

Suds chuckled, while Flush rolled his eyes. They gathered their things and promptly left for the library. Meanwhile, Captain Clean put his mask back on and HyJean set up a script on her computer to alert her of any mentions of sewers or toilet-related disappearances on social media.

'Right,' said the captain when he was ready, 'if you're ready to go I'll give The Driver a call.'

As grime fighting heroes, the squad often had to travel across the city to investigate various incidents. Since they couldn't afford their own car and the council were not willing to fund transport, they relied heavily on public transport or walking to grime scenes. For the longer trips, they used a regular taxi driver, although he wasn't a "regular" regular taxi driver. He was more of an "irregular" regular taxi driver.

The Driver, as he was simply known, was a young Indian man who had modified his car to drive at incredible speeds, faster than any formula one car. Despite his laid-back attitude, he was also an expert driver, so he could dodge traffic perfectly and had a remote control that his hacker brother had made to change the traffic lights at his will. The council had given him permission to use his extraordinary driving abilities to chauffer the Sanitary Squad around the city, as long as he drove normally at all other times. Which he did. Mostly.

'Hi, yeah, we need a lift,' said Captain Clean down the phone as they stood outside the community centre.

'I'll be there before you can say kaleidoscope,' said The Driver.

'Kaleidoscope?' the captain said in a puzzled tone.

As soon as he had finished saying the word, a car whooshed into the car park and pulled up with a loud screech. A window rolled down and The Driver said, 'Sorry I'm late.'

Captain Clean and HyJean set off in the taxi for the hospital, leaving Mary alone in her little office. Mary liked that she got to stay in the base on her own, because it meant she could play her music over the speakers. Today she opted for a bit of Black Sabbath.

💧💧

Filtham Hospital was one of those buildings that looked small from the outside, but seemed massive inside. With endless winding corridors, staircases and wards that led off to other private rooms, it was like someone had built an Ikea inside the TARDIS. It was also one of the few immaculately clean places in the city, although Captain Clean often argued the opposite. No matter how many hygiene certificates they received, he still found something to complain about. The staff had gotten so fed up of him complaining that they just started ignoring him, which was fine by the captain, as he wasn't very sociable anyway. But there was one doctor that he had known for many years and was friendly with.

'Steffi, good to see you,' said the captain as he entered the patient's room, heading straight for the antibacterial gel on the wall. He had used every single gel dispenser on the way in, partly to keep his hands clean, but mainly to check they were all working properly after his complaints following his previous visit.

'Thanks for coming, Captain,' said Doctor Steffi Scope as she handed him a clipboard with the patient notes on. 'I've never seen anything like this before.'

'I believe it's called a clipboard,' said the captain, gesturing to the clipboard. 'It's used for holding pieces of paper in place.'

'I meant this,' Steffi said, tutting as she closed the door behind them and drew back the curtain, revealing the patient lying sedated on the bed. He was a young man whose entire body seemed to be leaking. There were several buckets around his bed catching the water, and more around the room that were full.

'He was brought in a few days ago. His name is Nelson Spigot,' Doctor Scope explained. 'We don't know much about him. According to the police report, he's an orphan from America, moved here about a year ago. No registered address or employment history. As for his condition, his body is secreting impossible amounts of water. At first we thought it was sweat, but the tests all say it's just pure H_2O. We tried to draw bloods, but every time we did, the only thing that came out was water. We've done all kinds of scans, but this is beyond anything I learnt at medical school or watched on TV. I thought, since you and your team deal with a lot of… weird things, you might be able to help.'

The captain looked at HyJean who was staring at the patient with a mixture of awe and bemusement. After a minute alone to discuss it, HyJean told the doctor that they would take the case, but they would need to take the patient back to their base where they had more suitable equipment and facilities.

'We'd like to take him away to run some tests in our base,' explained HyJean.

'Take him away?' Doctor Scope replied.

'Thank you,' said the captain. 'That was easier than I expected.'

'No, I mean you can't take him away,' the doctor explained. 'We'd need to fill out lots of paperwork and get consent from the patient.'

'I don't think he'll mind; will you son?' said the captain, patting the now awake Nelson's arm. The patient responded with an indistinguishable gargled groan and the captain smiled. 'See, he loves the idea.'

'I'm still not sure, let me speak with my boss,' said Doctor Scope.

After explaining the situation and the squad's credentials to the senior doctors, it was agreed that they could take him - mainly because they didn't have a clue what else to do with him. Captain Clean and HyJean took Nelson back to their base, transporting him in a metal bathtub in the ambulance to contain the water. As they carried the bathtub through the ground floor of the community centre, the head of the receptionist peered up over her desk.

'Afternoon Captain,' she said with a well-rehearsed friendly smile.

'Yes, it is,' the captain replied, barely acknowledging her.

'What's up with him then?' the receptionist asked, gesturing to the unconscious water-soaked man in the bathtub.

The weird world of the squad would often pass through the community centre reception - a lot of which could have gotten them kicked out for breaking regulations - but fortunately the staff were very naïve and would believe any old excuse, and HyJean was now an expert at excuses.

'Uh, it's a charity thing,' HyJean lied. 'He's doing a sponsored tour of the city in a bathtub.'

'Ooh, well do let us know the details and I'll get the girls to do a whip round.'

'Will do. Thanks, Carol.'

In the base, a Nelson lay on a table in the shower room, where the water could run into the drains. It wasn't the most ideal place for a medical examination, but it was practical and – like every inch of the base – it was clean. However, as Jean turned to prepare her equipment, he slowly slid down the table and landed on the floor with a wet thud. Jean span around with a start. She offered to help Nelson up onto the table, but he insisted on doing it himself. He wearily dragged himself up and climbed on to the table as Jean continued to gather her equipment. However, before he could settle on the table, Nelson once again slid down the table and returned to the floor.

'Yeah, I might need some help actually,' he admitted.

After a few attempts, Jean eventually tied him down to keep him on the table. Nelson didn't say much about it, as the water pouring from his mouth made it difficult to speak and he was now in pain from falling.

When Jean started her tests, he said even less, because he was once again sedated. After hours of tests and experiments, Jean explained the situation to the captain and then woke Nelson to explain it to him.

'Okay, so based on the test results, you originally suffered from hyperhidrosis, which meant you sweated a lot anyway, but somehow it has been accelerated to an incredible rate. There were also a lot of unknown chemicals in your body which have diluted your blood to pure water. However, there are modified versions of the cells and minerals that blood usually contains, so your heart thinks this is normal and it's managing to pump the water around your body as if it were blood and it's performing all the same functions.'

'Okay, I didn't really understand any of that,' admitted Nelson. 'But you haven't said, why am I leaking all this water?'

'Um, well that's the thing see… I've no idea,' HyJean shrugged. 'I've done loads of tests and I've got a few theories, but it's just… impossible. It defies all the laws of physics and, to be honest, it's got me stumped.'

'Oh… okay,' said Nelson with a tone of disappointment in his voice. There was a long awkward silence, which he then broke. 'Can you help me?'

'I think so, yes,' said HyJean with a smile. 'You see, while I couldn't find out what's causing it, I was able to find a way to control it. If you'll allow me to demonstrate?'

She gestured to one of Nelson's arms and he nodded. She lifted it up into the air, watching as the droplets of water slowly dripped from it.

'So, your arm is leaking, but if I apply a little pressure,' she explained as she wrapped her hand around his wrist and squeezed gently. As it dangled there in the air, they all watched and were surprised to see the dripping stop. 'It stops the leaking. Not throughout your body, it seems to be localised to this arm. But I'm betting if we put something around both your wrists and ankles, it would cover your whole body and cancel the signal.'

'Really? Well, it's worth a try,' said Nelson, showing the hint of a smile for the first time since they'd met him.

'Excellent. And also… I still need to do a few more tests on you to check it will work, but I think I may be able to build a device that can control your leaking,' HyJean continued. After a little pause, she added, 'Control it enough to make you able produce water at will.'

'Why would I want to do that?' he asked.

'Well, that's what we wanted to talk to you about,' said the captain as he pulled up a wet chair and sat down beside the table with a squelch. He'd removed his mask so as not to intimidate the patient. 'From what Jean has told me, this cannot be fixed completely, but it can be controlled. If it is, you may be able to use it to your advantage.'

'What do you mean?'

'Well Nelson… we'd like you to join our squad.'

'What, are you guys like a pop group or something?'

'No, we fight grime.'

'Crime?'

'No, grime, as in sanitation themed crime. We ensure the city is safe and clean. There is evil out there, Nelson; criminals and psychopaths who want to bring down this city, creating chemical weapons and spreading viruses to wreak havoc.'

'Wait, what? How come none of this is in the news?' asked a startled Nelson.

'We try to keep a low profile,' the captain explained.

'Ha!' came a laugh from the other side of the base. It was laughed by Mary, who was currently typing up the seventh invoice that month for repairs to broken windows caused by the team.

'But we could really use someone like you on the team,' the captain continued. 'Sure, we've got technology and enthusiasm, but you've got actual super-powers. Jean reckons she can create something that will enable you to increase the volume of water and fire it like a jet. This doesn't have to be a burden, Nelson, you could do some real good.'

'Wait, so what you're saying is, you want me to become a superhero?' asked Nelson, sounding a little bemused.

'Well… yes,' said HyJean. 'But it's your decision and you need to think about it for a while, as there's a lot of danger and responsibility involved in –'

'Hell yeah!' Nelson cheered. 'Of course I'll do it.'

'Really?' asked a surprised HyJean.

'Lady, you had me at hyperhidrosis.'

'Excellent,' said the captain.

'Wait,' said Nelson as a thought suddenly occurred to him. 'I don't have to wear toilet roll on my head, do I?'

'No, that's my thing' said Captain Clean. 'Although you will have to have a shave; beards are terribly unhygienic.'

Meanwhile, in the public library, Flush and Suds - or Will and Mick, since they were dressed in their everyday attire so as not to attract any attention - waited at the reception desk for the librarian to return.

'I just don't like libraries,' whispered Will. 'They creep me out.'

'Really?' asked a surprised Mick. 'I know people don't like hospitals and cemeteries, but libraries?'

'Everyone's got to be so quiet here and it's all dark and dusty,' he explained. 'And they're letting you borrow books for free, what's that all about? Nobody gives you stuff for free these days. And did you see that librarian?'

'What about her?'

'She was so polite and happy, she's got to be hiding something.'

'Oh come on, she's just being friendly.'

'No she's not, she's –'

'Shh, here she comes.'

The librarian reappeared behind the desk wearing a smile that made Will furrow his brow in suspicion. She was a young woman, dressed smartly with glasses that made her look as intelligent as she was, and blonde hair that she wore in a bun. A name badge on her jumper – which she had seemingly made herself in an effort to make her appear less formal, decorated with drawings of hearts and flowers – identified her as Lily. She proudly presented two books: one quite old looking and the other much newer.

'Here you go sirs, The LoTech Story and An Architectural History of Filtham City. Are you going to check them out or would you like me to find you a table where you can read them?'

'We'd like to check them out please,' replied Mick.

'Certainly sir,' Lily nodded. 'Do you have your library card?'

'Oh, um…' Mick fumbled around, checking his pockets for his wallet, but to no avail. He turned to Will. 'Have you got yours?'

'Mick, I hate libraries. Why would I have a library card?'

'I'm afraid I can't let you take the books without a card,' said the librarian.

'Damnit, we'll have to go and come back,' Will sighed.

'Is there anything you can do?' asked Mick. 'The city is in terrible danger and our colleagues need to see these urgently. We don't really have time to go and come back. Please?'

Mick's polite plea seemed to trigger something in the librarian. She gestured for them to lean in close. 'I probably shouldn't do this, but if you can bring them back by the end of the day, I'll let you take them without scanning them.'

'Yes! That's bostin, thanks love,' said Will.

'You're a lifesaver,' said Mick, adding, 'possibly quite literally.'

Lily the librarian glanced around the room and handed them the books. She just hoped they'd bring them back. She'd done this several times before and gotten into quite a lot of trouble for it. The last time had been a man who'd borrowed a book about ancient Egypt, and when he'd failed to bring it back, Lily had tried to convince her boss that there was no such book. It didn't work, due to the pure coincidence that it was her boss that had written the book. She was suspended without pay for three weeks and eventually allowed to return. Meanwhile, the man who'd borrowed the book had travelled to Egypt and was now being worshiped as a modern-day pharaoh.

♦♦

Back in the base, HyJean and Mick studied the two books, looking for any clues that might lead them toward some answers. Meanwhile, Flush had noticed some water trickling out from the door to the shower room and wandered over. He inched the door open and peered inside.

'Uh guys, there's a man in here and I think he's really upset about something.'

'Oh, no, that's a patient from the hospital, we're looking after him,' said HyJean. 'Don't go in there, he's sleeping.'

'Well, it looks like he's having a wet dream,' Will said with a smirk.

Captain Clean explained to his colleagues about their trip to the hospital and the prospect of Nelson joining the squad.

'But who is he?' asked Suds.

'He's uh…' the captain started, suddenly realising that they knew very little about the American stranger that was currently lying in their shower room. 'We don't know. But he seems like a nice guy.'

'Well, at least now Mick won't be the biggest drip on the team,' joked Flush.

But before Suds could respond, HyJean cried out, 'I've got it!'

The squad all gathered around her as she showed them a page she'd found in An Architectural History of Filtham City.

'There's an old reservoir right under the LoTech building. It was damaged during the war, so they drained it and built a new reservoir a few miles away. This one was abandoned, but the LoTech building was built decades later, so whoever built it must've known about the old reservoir. But why connect the building to the reservoir if it's out of use?'

'I think I can answer that,' explained Suds. 'The architect of the LoTech building was one Jeremy Staines.'

'I don't like him already,' Captain Clean muttered.

'You're right not to,' said Suds. 'I looked him up and he made the news. Not long after the building was built, there were reports of technology going missing. Turns out a group of them were smuggling things out and selling them to competitors, and Staines was involved from the start. Nobody knew how it was done, but they discovered he'd added in those pipes so that they could send stuff down into a secret underground location – I'm guessing the reservoir – to avoid being caught.'

'Of course! The technology can't leave the building,' said HyJean. 'But if it goes under the building, it wouldn't pass any security scanners and would technically still be in the building.'

'Then they'd have time to figure out how to remove the chip so they could sell it,' added Suds.

'How did they catch them?' asked the captain.

'One of them put it down the wrong pipe and when the plumbers came out, they found the other pipes,' Suds explained. 'They blocked the pipes, but it seems like whoever's doing this has found a way to unblock them.'

'And now they're using the pipes to kidnap people,' Flush added as he caught up with what was going on.

'But Cap said the guy saw a hand,' Suds pointed out. 'How would someone get up the pipes and be strong enough to drag someone else down?'

'That's a good question,' said the captain. 'And one which we're going to find the answer to. Jean, is there an entrance to the reservoir?'

'Um, hang on,' she said, flicking through the pages. 'Yes, there's two, one either end. The nearest one is Reservoir Road.'

'Well, that figures. I always wondered why it was called that. Makes a lot more sense now,' said the captain turning to Suds. 'I suggest you take that one then.'

'Me?' he protested.

'Yes, we need to investigate the reservoir, but Jean and I have to look after our new friend.'

'Actually, I'm alright on my own if you want to go,' said HyJean.

'No, no. I need to stay and oversee his progress,' said the captain quickly, secretly keen to avoid the dirty walls and water of the underground. 'Suds, you can take Will with you though.'

'Oh bostin,' said Flush sarcastically. 'I'll get my wellies then, shall I?'

💧 💧

Underneath the streets of Filtham, Flush and Sergeant Suds made their way along the dark, dank tunnels of the secret underground reservoir. Their boots sloshed and squelched as they waded through the puddles of brown water that had dripped in through the cracks above. Rats scuttled by to check out the trespassers, eyeing them up for any valuables or cheesy comestibles. It was difficult to see much down there, but luckily Flush had brought a flashlight – or a "flushlight" as he insisted on calling it. They had very few self-branded tools and he couldn't resist the wordplay. He aimed it straight ahead and the light bounced off the curved walls and glistened on the dirty water, illuminating the endless damp corridor ahead.

'Jeez, it smells like my Nan's armpits down here,' said Flush.

'Did you smell her armpits often?' asked Suds.

'Well, she used to get us in headlocks all the time,' Flush explained. 'She was a tough old bird, big wrestling fan.'

As they turned a corner, Flush's light caught a rat that stared up at them. A surprised Suds quickly aimed his gun and fired it at the poor creature, soaking it in a big blob of pink goo.

'Dude, it's just a rat!' Flush pointed out.

'Oh, well… can never be too careful,' Suds said with a shrug as Flush reached down and wiped some of the goo away to free the startled rat, which ran off into the darkness.

They continued down the slimy, wet path and as they made their way around a bend, they suddenly saw something that shocked them as much as they'd shocked the rat. A man dressed in a white lab coat lay slumped against the wall, battered and bruised. His clothes were torn, and he had unusually large scratches on his face. But he didn't look upset about it. In fact, he showed no signs of life at all.

'That's an odd place to take a nap,' said Flush.

'I don't think he's sleeping,' said Suds as he took a closer look. 'I think he's dead.'

'Oh bugger, I hope not,' Flush replied. 'I'll check his pulse.'

Flush knelt down on the cold, watery floor and felt the man's wrist.

'Nothing,' he said, shaking his head with a mournful expression.

'Are you sure,' asked Suds.

'I dunno. Hang on, you hold this arm and I'll try the other one,' he said, handing Suds the detached limb he'd just been feeling. Suds looked at the severed arm with a mix of surprise and disgust.

'We've got a pulse!' cried Flush as he felt the man's other arm. 'He's still alive!'

'Phew. Quick, try and wake him up.'

'Hello! Mister, can you hear me?' asked Flush, tapping his cheek and shaking him roughly. But the man still lay motionless.

'Wait a minute, he's a man of science,' said Suds, before shouting, 'The theory of evolution has just been proven wrong!'

The man suddenly shot up with a startled gasp. He looked up at the two heroes that stood before him and muttered something in a panicked mumble.

'Calm down sir, we're here to help,' said Suds.

The man continued to mumble and stutter, scuttling about where he lay. He looked like a fish out of water, flopping about and babbling incoherently.

'Jeez, for a scientist he's not very literate is he,' said Flush.

The man suddenly started cowering as a dark shadow cast over him. He pointed up toward them.

'Alright,' said Flush, 'I know Suds is ugly, but he's not that bad.'

'N… n… no!' he stuttered and gestured to behind where they were standing. 'It's him!'

Flush and Suds turned around and to their surprise, they saw a giant creature – definitely humanoid in shape, but at least eight feet tall and skinnier than any fashion model. His bare, grey skin was rough and had little patches of a dark, mustard yellow in places. His face was grotesquely disformed, with a toothy sneer that made his face look like it was melting.

In a state of panic, Sergeant Suds whipped out what he thought was his gun, but was actually the man's dismembered arm, and pointed it towards the creature.

'Stay back,' he shouted, 'I'm armed!'

The creature lifted one of his own skinny arms, with long bony fingers that looked more like talons, and in one foul swoop, he sent the two heroes flying, bouncing off the wall and down into the murky waters. They lay motionless, just as the lab coated man had mere minutes ago.

💧💧

On the second floor of the community centre, HyJean was busy working away, still running tests on her patient. As she took samples of Nelson's blood – or whatever it was – and analysed it on the computer, she smiled to herself. It wasn't often she had an unconscious but handsome, naked man lying on a table for her. Although she was married, she still couldn't help but engage in a bit of fun flirting with her unconscious, undeniably good-looking patient.

'Well Mr Spigot, there's nothing wrong with your abs I see,' she giggled.

'Thanks doc,' Nelson said with a smile without opening his eyes.

HyJean jumped and let out a little squeal as she stumbled back and ran out of the room. Nelson chuckled to himself as he lay on the table in his half-conscious, hazy state and drifted back off to sleep.

💧💧

'Morning cocker,' said a cheery Flush, who'd clearly been awake for a while.

'Hm? What? Where are we?' asked a dazed Suds, looking around.

They were in a little alcove in a different part of the reservoir, both sat on chairs and tied to a large pipe that ran along the wall. It was better lit, and they could see there were computers dotted around the room outside, with people in tattered white lab coats operating them. Others were at desks, tinkering with little bits of metal components, or standing by a large, square, metal machine in the middle of the room, pressing buttons and taking notes. The people didn't look like they were there willingly. They whimpered and shook as they typed away and worked, like slaves, only better dressed.

'Slender Man over there captured us and tied us up,' Flush explained, gesturing to the giant grey monster who was pacing around. 'He's not very good at tying knots though. I wriggled free of mine a while ago, but I didn't want to leave you.'

'Thanks,' Suds said as he shuffled his hands and wriggled free of his own rope. 'You seem surprisingly calm about all this.'

'Not the first time I've woken up tied up in a stranger's home,' Flush said with a knowing grin. 'Right, shall we run?'

'No, wait. Let's see if we can get him talking first,' said Suds. 'Might as well try and find out what he's up to while we're here.'

'Good idea, leave this to me. I've got a way with people.'

'He doesn't look like people,' Suds said wearily.

Flush turned his attention to the creature who was now fiddling with the big machine.

'Excuse me mate!' Flush called, attracting the creature's attention. 'Alright mucker, how you doing? Looking very smart today, you're putting me to shame.'

The creature turned his head to them slowly. He looked confused and angry at being interrupted.

'Cut the flannel,' whispered Suds.

'Right, yes,' said Flush. 'So, my friend Suds and I - this is Suds here, say hello Suds.'

'Hello,' said Suds with a little wave, before suddenly realising he'd shown his untied hand and quickly whipping it behind his back in the hopes that the creature hadn't noticed.

'Ahem, so uh... my friend and I were wondering - we've got a little bet on whether you're human,' Flush continued. 'I think you are, but he reckons you're an alien. You're not an alien, are you?'

The creature slowly walked over to them, with long, heavy strides. Each step made a splash on the damp floor, echoing around the room. As he walked, his long, thin hands swung lazily by his side like two great pendulums.

'I was once human,' he said with a raspy but imposing voice. 'The lab experimented on me and made me into this. But I will have my revenge.'

'Right, I see, interesting,' said Flush. 'And how exactly will you get your revenge, if you don't mind me asking?'

The creature looked Flush straight in the eyes and its face contorted in an attempt to portray a sinister grin. Flush couldn't help but think it looked more like he was constipated.

'They brought me down here and abandoned me when their experiment failed. But I have been gathering people to construct this,' he said, pointing to the large machine in the middle of the room.

'Oh yes, that's a lovely bit of kit that,' said Flush.

'Very nice,' added Suds. 'But what does it do?'

'You will see soon enough. That is if you don't drown with the rest of the city.'

'Oh dear,' said Flush.

'That doesn't sound too good,' said Suds.

The creature gave a slightly breathy but very sinister cackle, leaning into both of them. They cowered back a little, which was more to do with the disgusting breath and flecks of spit that came from his mouth as he laughed than any kind of fear.

'Now silence, I must continue my work,' he said, turning to one of his workers. 'Sedate them.'

One of the white coated men came over and with an apologetic shrug he sprayed something in their eyes which made them suddenly feel very drowsy.

💧 💧

Suds groggily opened his eyes, his head aching and his vision blurry. As the room came into focus, he turned to address his fellow grime fighter. However, to his surprise, he found himself quite alone. At first, he panicked, thinking Limescale had taken Flush, but then he spotted a note stuck to the chair next to him, which he took off and read.

GONE TO GET THE OTHERS.
BACK SOON.
X

Meanwhile, back in the base, Flush was busy telling Captain Clean and HyJean what had happened over a bowl of cereal, which he had felt necessary to prepare before he filled them in, since he hadn't eaten in a while.

'So let me get this straight. This tall, grey man… creature, thing is capturing scientists to build some sort of machine and Mick is still trapped inside the reservoir?' asked Captain Clean.

'Yep,' said Flush. 'That's about the size of it.'

'What did he look like?' asked HyJean.

'He was a bit dazed when I left him, but I think he's alright,' Flush said as he munched on his cereal.

'Not Mick! The monster man,' the captain groaned.

'Oh! Sorry. He was like… a giant stick insect that had mated with an out-of-date Twiglet. Actually, I got a photo of him on the way out for Jargle, look,' said Flush, pulling up the photo on the phone to show the others.

'Lovely,' said HyJean with a grimace as the haunting face stared back at her.

'What on Earth is Jargle?' asked the captain.

'It's the latest social media app,' Flush explained. 'You post photos and add fun little captions.'

'You put a photo of a creature from the underground reservoir on your social media account?!' asked the captain.

'Of course not,' said Flush, with a slight pause before adding. 'I put it on the squad's account.'

'We have a Jargle account?' the captain asked Jean. He was rubbish with technology and did not see the point in social media, so he always relied on HyJean to fill him in with the latest news and online social movements.

'Apparently,' she shrugged. She was not surprised that this had happened, as Flush was always coming up with new ideas for the squad and the captain seemed to have very little interest in them, which would lead to Flush doing them anyway and the captain not being bothered to do anything about it.

'Anyway,' continued Flush, 'our followers chose the name Limescale as their favourite, so I think we should start calling him that.'

'What do you mean, chose?' asked the captain.

'Well, while I was on the bus coming back, I put a few suggestions on there. Sink Smasher, The Piper and Limescale. Y'know, 'cause Jean found all that limescale in the pipes.'

'I think they might be onto something,' said HyJean, who had been studying the photo closely. 'It was definitely limescale in the pipes, and it looks like he's covered in the same stuff.'

'So, he's covering himself in limescale? Or some kind of limescale suit?' asked the captain.

'No, I think it's part of him,' HyJean replied, zooming in on the photo. 'Look, there's no join, it looks organic.'

'Oh! Maybe that's how he's getting up through the pipes,' suggested Flush, as he started to piece together the parts of the puzzle in his head.

'Controlling the limescale, making it spread and using it to pull people down.'

'That seems a bit farfetched,' said the captain.

'Yes, but Martin Daley said that the victim didn't wash his hands before he was taken,' said HyJean, with a sudden burst of energy at the emerging realisation. 'I think Flush is right. It's all starting to make sense now.'

'Does it?' asked Flush.

'Yes, this… Limescale,' she said, making sure to do air quotes when she said the name to show she thought it was a silly idea to name the villain, 'he's been coming up the pipes in various places and taking people. The limescale – the stuff, not the creature – can grow up the pipe and snatch people. Think about it, the first time it happened, the water had been turned off. The second time, he didn't wash his hands and probably stayed at the sink a little too long. Mr Daley said that the victim liked to check himself out in the mirror. Maybe the water was keeping it at bay.'

'Yeah, if the pipes were connected at some point along the way, then the water would've made it harder for the limescale to grow,' added Flush.

'Another perfect example why you should always wash your hands,' said the captain. 'If this man had washed his hands, he might still be alive.'

'He is still alive,' Flush pointed out. 'Limescale's got him working down in the reservoir.'

'Right, yes, of course,' said the captain, now pacing around overexcitedly. 'So, what is Limescale planning?'

'I don't really know, he didn't tell us anything useful,' admitted Flush.

'Well, what did he say?' HyJean pressed.

'He did say he was going to use this machine of his to flood the city.'

'I think that's pretty useful information,' HyJean said, a little frustrated.

'This is serious,' said the captain in a slightly worried tone. 'We have to stop him.'

'And rescue Suds and the kidnapped people,' added HyJean.

'Yes, I suppose we can do that as well,' agreed the captain. 'Right, we'll do a two-pronged attack. I'll go down on the north side and try to distract him, while you two go down on the south side and rescue Suds and the others.'

'What about the drip?' Flush said, gesturing towards the shower room.

'He'll be okay for a few hours,' said HyJean, who was walking off to her own room to clip some useful sprays and` things onto her utility belt. 'I've got some extra-strong tranquiliser. We should be able to use that to take

Limescale down.'

'Okay, cool. I'll just finish this and then we'll get off,' Flush said, gesturing to his half-full bowl of cereal.

Captain Clean grabbed the bowl and threw it in a nearby bin. Flush sat shocked and pouted a little like a spoilt child who'd just had his favourite toy taken away.

'There, you're finished,' the captain said. 'Now come on.'

💧 💧

'Urgh, it's filthy down here. Someone should really come down and clean this place up,' said Captain Clean as he made his way through the dark, murky tunnels. He winced as he took each step, wading through a stream of what looked like sewage water. He shone his torch ahead, the light bouncing off the curved walls and glistening on the dirty water, illuminating the corridor ahead. As the captain moved further down, the light caught one of the reservoir rats, which looked startled and scuttled away, like it was expecting to be pelted by a blob of pink goo in the same way that they had heard their ratty friend had been attacked earlier that day. The captain let out a little squeal at the sight of the rat and was glad that nobody was around to witness it.

Meanwhile, HyJean and Flush were making their way through their own tunnel, Flush leading the way as he confidently lied about remembering which way he'd come when he had escaped. In truth, he'd been so busy running away that he hadn't bothered to remember the path he took. Eventually they passed a wall that he recognised, which was surprising, given how similar everywhere looked.

'Right, it's just down there,' Flush said, pointing to a corner where flickering lights reflected off the walls. As they crept closer, they heard the faint hum of machinery and noises of people working.

'Okay, let's wait here. Cap said he'll text me when he's in position,' HyJean said. They waited for a while, and sure enough, less than a minute later, her phone vibrated with a text message from the captain. There were no words, just one worried looking emoji.

'Is that the signal?' asked Flush.

'Must be,' HyJean shrugged. Let's go.'

They cautiously poked their heads around the corner and scanned the room. There was no sign of Limescale, just several dishevelled people nervously working at the computers. Captain Clean must have drawn him out, they thought. HyJean gave a nod and Flush quickly and quietly made his way over to where Sergeant Suds was being held, while she headed to the nearest person working at a computer - who just so happened to be Victor Timm.

'Shh, we're here to help,' whispered HyJean, holding up a finger to gesture for him to keep quiet.

'Oh, thank god,' whispered Victor nervously. 'I haven't a clue what I'm doing with this, I'm just tapping away and hoping he doesn't notice.'

'It's okay, Captain Clean is distracting Limescale while we help everyone escape,' she explained. 'You go and I'll get the others.'

Victor Timm thanked her and joyously left his cold, damp prison. On the other side of the room, Flush was busy untying his friend, whose hands had been tied tighter after being sedated.

'Why did you go without me?' asked a disgruntled Sergeant Suds.

'Well, you were sleeping and you looked comfy, so I didn't want to wake you,' said Flush. 'Anyway, how've you been?'

'Oh, just fine thanks,' Suds replied sarcastically. 'Aside from the freezing cold draft, the starvation and the constant threat of being killed by a giant raging monster, it's been just spiffing.'

'Alright, I said I was sorry.'

'No you didn't!'

'Okay, well I'm sorry. Now keep your voice down.'

As Flush worked on the ungiving knot, there came a tumultuous grumble that echoed around the reservoir.

'Blimey, you really are hungry,' said Flush.

'You!' bellowed the familiar booming voice of Limescale.

'You said that without moving your lips,' said Flush, still looking at Suds. 'How did you do that voice?'

As a look of panic grew on Suds' face and an eerie shadow loomed over him, Flush gulped at the sudden realisation.

'You are trying to escape,' Limescale continued.

Flush turned around and, despite being terrified, tried not to be intimidated by the towering, flaky figure. 'Actually, I've already gone and come back, mate. Did you not miss me?'

Evidently, Limescale did not take kindly to being taunted, and once again his large, vine-like arm swooped down on them. Flush dived out of the way and Suds' chair was knocked over, with Suds still partly tied to it.

Flush grabbed the chair that he had once been tied to and swung it at the rampaging monster, adding a cry of, 'Take a seat!'

It was not quite as good a weapon as he had hoped. The chair smashed into pieces and barely had any effect on Limescale.

'Well, that worked,' groaned Suds, lying sideways on the floor.

Back in the main part of the reservoir, HyJean was alerted to the noise coming from across the room. Hoping the boys could keep Limescale distracted for a while, she looked around to find the captain, who she assumed must have been helping the kidnapped victims or sabotaging the machine. However, she quickly learnt that Captain Clean was actually nowhere to be seen. She tried calling him on the phone, but there was no signal.

'Typical,' she muttered to herself, before heading over to join in the fight.

By the time she got there, Suds had gotten free of his restraints and had recovered his soap gun, which Limescale had carelessly left nearby. Flicking it to the highest setting, Suds fired it at Limescale's grotesque face. With relative ease, the creature just wiped the pink goo off his face and flung it at Suds, who dodged it. However, it did give HyJean a window of opportunity to attack. She pulled out a spray bottle and started spraying it all over Limescale, who roared loudly as his body began to sizzle and burn, bits of his flaky skin peeling off and falling away.

'What was that stuff?' shouted Flush as he dodged Limescales flailing arms.

'Non-ionic surfactants!' HyJean replied.

'I repeat, what was that stuff?' Flush shouted back, a little more irritably.

'It's used to get rid of limescale,' she explained. 'It should weaken him at least.'

As Limescale's body continued to shed itself of the limescale, flakes peeling off and drifting to the floor like passengers jumping off a sinking ship, he became noticeably weaker – his movements slowed and his attacks had less power behind them. The grime fighters danced around, avoiding the swipes and jabs for a short while as their attacker weakened, until at last they nodded and attacked in unison. Flush whipped out his whip and swung it around Limescale's legs, expertly typing them together; Suds took a running jump and tackled him down onto the floor with a great thud; and HyJean stabbed him with the sedative she'd prepared. They pinned the creature down and watched as he wriggled and writhed, splashing about in the small puddles of dirty water like a fish at a rave, and then gradually settled until he lay still.

'That wasn't actually too difficult,' said Flush with a smile as he stood up and wiped his hands.

'I know,' agreed Suds. 'We must be getting better.'

As if on cue, there came the sound of splashing footsteps and Captain Clean ran into the room, panting as if he'd just finished running a marathon. With his adrenaline levels already high, Suds reacted instinctively and span around, throwing a punch at the captain's face and knocking him to the ground with a splash.

'Oh crap,' Suds said when he realised who it was he'd punched. He reached down and helped the captain up. 'Sorry Cap, didn't realise it was you.'

'No worries,' he said, using his cape to wipe his aching face. He gestured down at Limescale. 'You stopped him then?'

'We sure did,' said Flush proudly.

'And where have you been exactly?' asked HyJean.

'I uh… I got lost,' the Captain replied between pants, a little embarrassed.

'Why are you so dirty?' asked Suds.

'I was... in the sewers,' he mumbled.

'What?'

'I was in the sewers, okay!' he shouted. 'I went down the wrong manhole and ended up wandering about in the sewers.'

'Didn't you have your tracker app on?' asked HyJean, referring to an app she'd made for the squad that allowed them to see each other's whereabouts.

'I thought I could navigate myself,' the captain argued. 'Look, it doesn't matter, I'm here now. What's the situation?'

'We nearly got killed because you cocked up the plan,' said Flush.

'Very helpful, thank you Flush,' the captain replied.

'We've sedated Limescale, but we've no idea what this machine does,' explained HyJean, pointing to the big machine in the middle of the room, which had suddenly sprung to life, with lights flashing and gears grinding. The computer monitors were also in a frenzy, with graphs and text flashing all over the screen.

While the others checked out the machine, HyJean wandered over to one of the computers. It didn't make much sense to her, but suddenly the screen changed and several elements on it turned green, with "complete" notices indicating that the machine was now fully functioning and ready to do immeasurable damage.

'Um, guys. This doesn't look good,' HyJean said, calling them over.

'Oh bugger,' said Flush. 'What's it doing?'

'I've got no idea, I've never seen anything like this before,' said HyJean. 'But I'm guessing it's activated and ready to flood the city.'

'Yeah, that's definitely in the not good category,' said Suds.

'Right, let's figure this out,' said Captain Clean. 'HyJean, take a look at the computers, see if you can shut it down. Flush, try and wake Limescale, see if we can get some answers out of him. Suds, help get those last couple of guys out. I'll see if I can turn this thing off.'

HyJean rushed over to the row of computers, tapping at the keys, but after being abandoned for a while, the computers had gone into standby mode and required a password to get back in. HyJean typed RESERVOIR1 and hit enter. Nothing. RESERVOIR2. Nothing. RESERVOIR3. After a few more attempts at increasing numbered intervals, she suddenly had an idea. PASSWORD. It worked! She was in.

'When will they learn?' she muttered as she skimmed through everything on the screens and frantically began tapping and clicking to try and stop the process.

Meanwhile, Flush was busy slapping Limescale on the cheeks. 'Helloooo! This is your morning wakeup call! Come on you stupid great twig, wake up!' He leaned down and shouted into his ear, 'WAKE UP! WE NEED YOUR HELP! WAKE UP DAMN YOU!'

Due to his size and abilities, HyJean had used an extra strong tranquiliser, which was proving very effective, as Limescale lay perfectly still, not even flinching. While his colleagues were trying their best to find answers and get people to safety, Captain Clean was pacing around next to the machine. Back and forth, back and forth, muttering to himself.

'What do I do? What do I do?' he asked himself repeatedly. In a moment of frustration, he kicked the machine.

It clanked and whirred loudly and then… it stopped. The lights flickered off. The dials slumped down to zero. The whole machine fell silent, and the computers turned red and stated the machine was inactive.

'It's stopped,' said a bemused HyJean. 'But… how?'

'I found a way to uh… reroute the circuits to reverse the polarity of the…' the captain began.

'You kicked it didn't you?' she said with a frown.

'Yes,' he said with an embarrassed nod.

They had done it. They'd stopped the machine and saved the city from being flooded, as well as capturing the monster behind the evil plan.

'Nice work,' said Suds, as he joined them by the machine.

At which point Flush's efforts suddenly paid off and Limescale burst to life, roaring and thrashing about. Flush flew off him and tumbled onto the floor with a thud. The three remaining grime fighters ran over and HyJean managed to sedate Limescale again.

'We should call the police before he wakes up again. There's no signal here though,' said HyJean, turning to Captain Clean. 'You go and call them, if you can manage that, and we'll wait here.'

The captain took out his phone, but as he was about to leave, he paused. There was a noise. An echoey noise in the distance. He looked at HyJean. She had clearly heard it too and was looking around the room. The noise grew. It sounded like someone screaming. Then suddenly, Chief Inspector Dovedale came flying out of a large pipe hole in the ceiling that was coated with bits of limescale. He landed in the dirty water with a splash and a thud, causing the others to jump back a little in surprise. As he pulled himself up and brushed himself off, Dovedale looked around at the grime fighters.

'What are you lot doing here?' he asked. 'Where's the monster?'

The grime fighters all silently pointed to Limescale, who was still lying unconscious on the floor.

'Oh. I'd come down here to stop him,' said the inspector, sounding a little disappointed. 'We just figured out where the pipes lead.'

'We've already stopped him,' said HyJean, trying not to sound too smug, but inside she was blowing a triumphant raspberry at the Chief Inspector.

'That was a cool entrance though,' said Flush, leaning in and giving him a thumbs up. 'I definitely want a go of that.'

'Right, well I'll call my men and have him taken away then,' said Dovedale. 'We'll get this place sealed up too.'

'Aww, I was thinking we could use it as a new base,' said Flush. 'It'd be cool, like the Batcave.'

'Absolutely not, it's filthy down here,' said the captain sternly, holding up his hands in an X shape. 'And it's infested with rats.'

'Oh come on, they're not that bad,' said Suds, who had picked up one of the rats and held it out towards Captain Clean.

The captain squealed and cowered from it, shouting for Suds to put the filthy rodent down and get it away from him. But, in good spirits from their latest victory, Suds instead started chasing the captain around the old reservoir, teasing him with the rat while the others watched and laughed.

💧💧

The next day, the male members of the squad, along with Mary, were gathered in the base discussing their new recruit.

'Have you found out what happened to him?' asked Suds, gesturing to the room where Nelson had been kept.

'He remembered he was a volunteer test subject at some lab, but he can't remember much else,' said Captain Clean. 'Whatever they did to him, it seems to have affected his memory.'

'Wait, Limescale said some guys in a laboratory made him look like that,' said Flush. 'Maybe it's the same lab?'

'Maybe. I'll look into it,' said the captain. 'We also need to find him somewhere to stay temporarily.'

'He can stay with me,' said Flush keenly. 'I've always wanted a flatmate, and it'll keep the water bill down if he doesn't need to shower. Do you reckon his water is drinkable?'

'Don't ask him that, dear,' said Mary. 'The poor boy's been through enough, without you turning him into a walking water cooler.'

Before they could discuss it further, HyJean entered and gestured for them to be quiet.

'He's ready,' she said.

The squad all turned their attention to her direction, and she beckoned for Nelson to come into the room. As he entered, the squad were surprised to see that he was no longer leaking. Dressed in just a pair of trunks with a pair of metal gauntlets on his wrist and a nervous smile on his face. The rest of the squad gave a little cheer.

Captain Clean stood up and shook Nelson's hand, 'Good to see you so dry.'

'Yo, Nelson! You look bostin mate,' said Flush.

'Thanks,' said Nelson with an appreciative little nod.

'How do you feel?' asked Suds.

'Much better, thanks,' Nelson smiled.

'Now all he needs is an alias,' said Catain clean, sitting back down at the table.

'Why does he need a book of maps?' asked Flush.

'No, an alias,' said Suds. 'A name he'll go by as a grime fighter.'

'He's got a name,' said Flush. 'He's The Drip.'

'We're not calling him The Drip!' said the captain.

'What about Moist Man?' suggested Mary.

Flush burst out laughing at this suggestion and HyJean couldn't help but giggle too. Suds gently patted his wife's arm and said, 'No love, that sounds wrong.'

'What about something more literal, to do with turning the water on and off like a tap?' suggested HyJean.

'Hm, I like the idea, but The Tap doesn't sound very authoritative,' said the captain.

'Well in America, we don't call them taps, we call them faucets,' said Nelson.

'Faucet huh?' said the captain thoughtfully.

The squad all looked at each other and each of them smiled.

'What, is that like a rude word over here or something?' asked Nelson, confused by their reaction to the name.

'No,' said HyJean. 'No, it's not.'

'But it sounds like a perfect name for a grime fighter,' said Captain Clean.

'Really? You like it?' asked Nelson.

They all nodded in unison.

'Awesome,' he smiled. He punched the palm of his hand with his fist and in the coolest voice he could muster said, 'Well in that case… hi, I'm Faucet!'

For more good, clean fun
go to sanitarysquad.com